THE FI MONSTER

Steve Barlow and Steve Skidmore
Illustrated by Garry Davies

"**A**aarr!" roared the big, hairy monster.

Simon giggled. "I love monsters," he said. "Especially the blue one!"

It was holiday time. Simon and his sister, Ellie, were watching their favourite monster film.

"I like the ugly one," said Ellie. "It reminds me of you!"

Before Simon could reply, his mum stormed into the lounge. She picked up the remote control and switched off the television. The monsters disappeared.

"Oh, Mum!" cried Simon and Ellie.

"Don't 'oh, Mum' me!" Their mum looked very annoyed. "Which one of you two has been in the fridge?" she asked.

Simon looked at Ellie. Ellie looked at Simon. They both looked at Mum and shrugged.

"I want to know which one of you little monsters has been in the fridge?" repeated Mum. "And I want to know now!"

Ellie smiled. "It must have been Simon," she said, cheekily. "I'm much bigger than he is. I can't fit into the fridge!"

"Neither can I," said Simon. "There are too many shelves in it!" The children began to giggle.

"This isn't a laughing matter!" snapped Mum, pointing at them both.

Ellie and Simon shut up immediately. They put on their best 'Mum-is-telling-us-off' faces.

"Who has been taking things out of
the fridge without asking?" asked Mum.

"What sort of things?" asked Simon.

"The apple pie we were going to have
for pudding!" said Mum. "It's gone. One of
you two has eaten it, and I want to know
which one it was!"

Ellie and Simon realised that their mum was in a serious mood. This was no time for joking. It was time for blaming each other.

"It wasn't me!" said Ellie. She pointed at Simon. "It must have been him."

"It wasn't me!" said Simon. He pointed at Ellie. "It must have been her."

"Stop arguing," ordered Mum. "If you won't tell me, there's no pudding for either of you!" She stomped out of the room.

Ellie looked at Simon. "I know I didn't take the pie. It must have been you." She began to chant,

"Simon, Simon, you ate all the pie, man.
Simon, Simon, you ate all the pie, man."

"No I didn't," said Simon. "Stop saying that, Ellie!"

That night, the family sat down for dinner. They had pasta. They had salad. They didn't have any pudding.

"I'd have liked some apple pie," said Dad. "If only some little monster hadn't eaten it all!"

Ellie folded her arms. "It wasn't me."

"And it wasn't me!" said Simon.

Mum put up her hand. "Don't start that nonsense again."

Ellie and Simon scowled at each other.

"Ah well," sighed Dad. "I'll have a glass of orange juice instead." He got up and went to the fridge.

Dad opened the fridge door. He reached in for the orange juice bottle and took it out. His eyes opened wide. "It's empty! Who drank all the juice?"

Before Simon or Ellie could say anything, Mum held up her hand.

"I don't want to hear any excuses. That bottle was full earlier. Which one of you drank it?" She looked Simon in the eye. "Was it you?"

Simon shook his head. "No, Mum, honestly."

Mum looked Ellie in the eye. "Was it you?"

Ellie shook her head. "No, Mum.
Cross my heart and hope to die."

Simon waited for Ellie to drop down
dead for telling such a fib. But she didn't.

"This is ridiculous," said Dad. "First the
apple pie disappears and now the juice.
They can't just vanish into thin air. One of
you must have taken them." He pointed to
the door. "Until you tell me the truth, you
can both go to your rooms!"

Ellie and Simon trudged up the stairs, moaning.

"This is all your fault," said Ellie.

"No it isn't," said Simon. "I didn't take anything. If you think it was me, then you're strange!"

Ellie stood by her bedroom door. "I'm not the strange one. You are!" She began chanting,

*"Simon's strange, Simon's strange,
he drank all the orange."*

"No I didn't," said Simon. "And that's a rubbish chant. Orange and strange don't rhyme. Hah!"

Ellie curled her lip. "Nothing rhymes with orange. That's what our teacher told us. Anyway, you must be strange. No one else would eat a whole apple pie and drink a bottle of orange." With a final "Huh!" Ellie marched into her room and slammed the door shut.

"I didn't do it," whispered Simon. "I'll prove it was you."

The next day, Simon wasn't feeling very well. "My tummy hurts," he told his mum.

"That's because you ate the pie and drank the orange," said Ellie.

"I didn't," said Simon. But his mum was looking at him suspiciously.

"Ellie and I are going to see Grandma," she said. "You can stay at home with your dad. He's doing some odd jobs in the garden."

She wagged a warning finger. "There's a chocolate cake in the fridge. It had better still be there when I come home."

"It will be," said Simon, "because Ellie's not going to be here."

"Ha ha!" said Ellie, sticking out her tongue.

Simon said nothing. But all the time Ellie and his mum were out, he kept an eye on the fridge.

Later that afternoon, when Mum and Ellie arrived back home, Simon was feeling better.

"I'm hungry now, Mum," he said.

"So am I," said Dad. "Let's all have some chocolate cake."

"Good idea," said Mum. She opened the fridge door, looked in, and gave a gasp. "The cake!"

Simon hurried to the fridge and looked in. The chocolate cake was nowhere to be seen! Only a few dark crumbs remained on the cake plate.

"Oh, Simon," said his mum. "Not again!"

"I haven't had it!" said Simon. "I've had a tummy ache!"

Ellie started to chant,

"*Simon's got a tummy ache,*
'cos he ate the chocolate cake."

Simon shook his head. "It wasn't me!"

"Well, it couldn't have been Ellie," said Mum. "She's been with me all day." She shook her head sadly. "Simon, if you want something to eat or drink, there's no need to steal. You only have to ask."

"I didn't steal anything!" insisted Simon. A thought struck him. "Maybe it was a monster – like in the film. Maybe this monster lives in our fridge!"

There was a moment's silence. Then Ellie began to hoot with laughter.

"A fridge monster! You're the only monster around here!"

Even Simon's mum and dad started to chuckle. Tears sprang to Simon's eyes.

"I'll show you!" he said, running out of the kitchen. "I'll show you!"

Simon spent the evening in his room, thinking up a plan. He was going to prove that he wasn't the thief!

He waited until his parents had gone to bed and then waited a bit longer. Soon, he heard his dad's snores. It was time for action! Carefully, Simon crept out of his room. He tip-toed down the stairs and headed towards the kitchen.

Moonlight streamed in through the kitchen window.

"Right," Simon muttered. "Now for the bait."

He opened a cupboard and took out a packet of biscuits. Then he found a plate and tipped the biscuits onto it. "Let's see who the thief really is," he whispered to himself.

Simon opened up the fridge. Carefully, he placed the plate of biscuits on a shelf and shut the door. Then, he opened the door to the cupboard under the sink and climbed in. He tucked up his knees and pulled the door shut.

It was very dark inside. Simon wondered whether his plan would work.

He had no idea how long he waited. He was just dropping off to sleep, when he heard a crunching, munching noise. Someone was eating the biscuits!

Simon flung the cupboard door open. "Got you!" he yelled.

But the kitchen was empty!

Simon looked around. The sound was coming from inside the fridge!

He took a deep breath and grabbed hold of the fridge door handle. He pulled the door open – and cried out in shock. He couldn't believe his eyes!

Sitting on a shelf, noisily chomping the biscuits, was a green and purple hairy … thing!

It had a low forehead, and little piggy eyes, and a mouth that was so wide it looked as if it ought to meet at the back of its head! The creature looked up.

"What do you want?" it said, gruffly. "Can't you see I'm eating?"

"What are you?" asked Simon in a trembling voice.

The creature gave a loud burp. Crumbs fell from its mouth. "What does it look like I am?" it said. "I'm a fridge monster!"

"I knew it!" cried Simon. "You're the one that's been stealing the food and drink!"

"So what?" said the hairy creature. "That's what we fridge monsters do."

Simon pointed an accusing finger at the fridge monster. "Did you eat the apple pie and the cake?"

The monster smacked its lips. "Oh yes," it said.

Simon scowled. "I got the blame for eating them."

"Tough luck!" said the monster. "They were very yummy. Especially the cake. Can I have some more?"

"No," said Simon, "you can't. You've eaten it all."

The fridge monster sighed. "Oh well, I'll have to see what's left in the fridge next time."

At that, Simon lost his temper.

"Oh no you won't!" he shouted. "I'm tired of getting the blame for stealing the food you've been eating. I'm telling my mum and dad about you!"

Simon slammed the fridge door shut. He rushed upstairs and into his parents' bedroom. "Mum, Dad! Get up!"

After a minute or two of shouting, Simon managed to get his parents out of bed. Bleary-eyed, they followed him into the kitchen. Ellie came down too, to see what all the fuss was about.

"I'll show you who's really been stealing our food!" cried Simon in triumph. He flung open the fridge door with a flourish.

Wide-eyed, his parents and Ellie looked into the fridge, staring open-mouthed at …

… nothing.

Simon couldn't believe his eyes. There was nothing there! Just an empty plate covered with a few biscuit crumbs.

"But … but … there was a fridge monster in there five minutes ago," protested Simon. "I saw it!"

Ellie cackled.

"Simon's seeing monsters,
Simon's going bonkers …"

Then Simon's mum started shouting
about naughty boys who wake people up
in the middle of the night for no reason at
all. And Simon's dad started shouting
about silly boys who make up stories
about monsters that aren't there …

But Simon wasn't listening. He was
thinking about the monster.

"If it eats fridge
food," he thought,
"then it must have
gone somewhere else
to find it. And if it's not
in OUR fridge any
more …

... then maybe it's in YOUR fridge!"